The
DRUMMER
BOY

by Philemon Sturges
illustrated by Tyrone Geter

 HOUGHTON MIFFLIN   BOSTON

IT WAS 1776. Eliza Potter lived on Ferry Point Farm in Bristol, Rhode Island. She lived with her mother, her older brother, John, and her uncle, Captain Simon Potter. She helped tend geese, grow onions, and make sails for boats.

Eliza liked her chores. But most of all, she liked to sit on Seal Rock. She loved to watch ospreys dive into the sparkling water. She often saw a boy sailing a model boat on the opposite shore, and they waved to each other.

A few times each year, Eliza and John loaded a boat with onions. Then they rowed down to Newport Harbor to sell them. "Everyone loves our Bristol onions," said John. "That's mighty good for us!"

Newport had one of the very best harbors in the Colonies. It was filled with tall ships. John loved the tall ships. He was a good carpenter, and he often helped to repair them.

Thomas Strand lived just across the water from Eliza and John. His father was the commander of the British soldiers in Newport. Thomas was the drummer boy in his father's regiment.

Thomas liked living in the British army camp. And he enjoyed marching to the beat of his own drum. But most of all he liked making model boats. Back home in England, his model boats had won prizes. Thomas still sailed one of his boats when he had free time. It usually caught a brisk southwest wind and sped toward Seal Rock on the opposite shore. Sometimes he saw a girl sitting on Seal Rock, and they waved to each other.

Thomas and his father often rowed over to Bristol to have a look around. Thomas hoped to meet the girl who waved, but he never did.

Like Newport Harbor, Bristol Harbor was full of tall ships. "The ones over there belong to Captain Simon Potter, the Patriot leader," said Thomas's father. "I'm sure that he and his men are planning something. They say you can't trust those Patriots."

"Is that why we're here in the Colonies, because we can't trust the Patriots?" Thomas asked.

"In a way," said his father. "We're keeping order in the Colonies, and we have our hands full. The Patriots don't like being told what to do by King George. I won't be surprised if soon there is a war between Britain and the Patriots."

Thomas's father was right. In July 1776, the British and the Patriots went to war. In August, British ships sneaked into Bristol Harbor. They burned down Captain Potter's ships, a church, and several houses.

But the Patriots had spirit and energy. They were not discouraged. Soon Captain Potter began to build a new ship. John and Eliza had to help their uncle. John did some of the carpentry. Eliza and her mother sewed the sails. It was very hard work. When they complained a bit to their mother, she said, "It's for the cause of liberty."

Meanwhile, back in Newport at the British army camp, Thomas's father was getting ready to march. He said to Thomas, "King George has ordered us to destroy any ships that Captain Potter is building. And our spies tell us that he is building one near Bristol Harbor. We've got to hurry!"

Thomas put on his bright red uniform. His drum rolled smartly as he and his father led the soldiers to Newport Harbor. There they boarded a twenty-gun ship and sailed off toward Bristol.

The soldiers landed just north of Bristol Harbor. With Thomas in front, the soldiers marched toward the boatyard in which Captain Potter's ship was being built. As he drummed, Thomas admired the bright red coats all around him.

Now I know why the Patriots call us Lobsterbacks, he thought. Thinking about lobsters made Thomas hungry. He was tired too. It was a long, long march.

At the Potter boatyard, all of the carpenters were busy. Eliza and her mother had gone home to make lunch for the hungry crew.

Suddenly someone cried out, "The Lobsterbacks are coming!" But it was too late. When John looked over the side of the unfinished boat, he saw British soldiers coming his way. They were led by a drummer boy about his own age.

The soldiers captured John and his shipbuilding friends. They set the ship and the boatyard on fire. Then they began marching their prisoners back toward the British ship north of Bristol Harbor.

For Thomas, the march back to the British ship seemed much longer than the march toward the Potter boatyard. He had long since passed from hungry and tired to thirsty, hot, and exhausted. No one seemed to notice that his drumming had stopped and he was falling behind.

John was more angry and frightened than tired. He felt a bit better when he realized that the soldiers were headed in the direction of his home, Ferry Point Farm.

When the soldiers and their prisoners got to Ferry Point Farm, Eliza and her mother were standing next to the barn. The soldiers were so tired that they decided to rest there for a while. The commander told Eliza and her mother to bring water for the soldiers. At first Eliza and her mother didn't want to help the soldiers in any way. But then a young Lobsterback boy fainted right in front of them. Eliza ran to get him some tea and some bread with honey.

Thomas's father bent down to see what had happened to his son.

When Thomas opened his eyes, he saw his father and then Eliza. They recognized each other from all the times they had waved across the water.

First Thomas ate a bit and had a sip of tea. Then he said to Eliza, "Thank you. I hope no one has been hurt. I meant no harm to anyone. If fact, when the war stops, I want to stay in Bristol and work on boats."

"I wish my brother was here to talk to you," said Eliza. "He's a skilled carpenter and he works on boats."

19

"I am here," said John, to his sister's surprise. "But I've been taken prisoner."

"Why have you taken my son?" John's mother asked Thomas's father.

"It was King George's order," he answered.

"Well, I'm sure King George would be pleased that we have taken care of your son," said Eliza hopefully. "I know he would want to reward us by setting my brother free."

"I'm not sure about King George, but I will release your brother," said Thomas's father.

Later that day, John and Eliza gave Thomas a ride home in their rowboat. He was too tired to march back to the ship.

"Thank you," said Thomas to John and Eliza. "When the war is over, John, I will come back and learn shipbuilding from you."

"I'd like that," said John.

"Me too," said Eliza.

Thomas did indeed move to Bristol after the American Revolution. His children and grandchildren built some of the fastest boats the world has ever seen.